THIS BLOOMSBURY BOOK

BELONGS TO

....

For Grandman – G.A.

For Philippa – S.H.

BLOOMSBURY
CHILDREN'S
BOOKS

First published in Great Britain in 2003 by Bloomsbury Publishing Plc
36 Soho Square, London, W1D 3QY
This paperback edition first published in 2004

A CIP catalogue record of this book is available from the British Library

ISBN 0 7475 6479 5
ISBN-13 9780747564799

Printed in Belgium by Proost

3 5 7 9 10 8 6 4 2

All papers used by Bloomsbury Publishing are natural, recyclable products made from wood grown in well-managed forests.
The manufacturing processes conform to the environmental regulations of the country of origin.

My Grandson is a Genius!

by Giles Andreae

illustrated by Sue Hellard

BLOOMSBURY
CHILDREN'S
BOOKS

My grandson is a genius!
It's plain for all to see,
I'm sure it won't be long
Before he sits for a degree.

I know he's only two years old
But when you watch him play,
It's obvious he'll be
A famous scientist one day.

And although it sounds unlikely,
If you heard my grandson speak,
You'd probably elect him
As Prime Minister next week.

He's clearly very musical,

'Cause when he's in his cot,
He wriggles to the rhythm
Of Puccini's Turandot.

And when you see him walking

It's embarrassingly clear

That he'll be in the Olympics
Not much later than next year.

He moves so very gracefully
For such a tender age,

3 ITEMS ONLY

And his voice is so angelic

That he'll really suit the stage.

His paintings are so masterful
You couldn't fail to tell
That my grandson and Picasso
Would have got on very well.

And when he kicks a football

You'd be hard put to deny

That any player ever

Has had such a brilliant eye.

Though I'm not much one for boasting,

If you saw his little face,
You'd agree that they should use him
To promote the human race.

Yes, my grandson is a genius
And, though I'm not sure I'd agree,
His parents sometimes say
That he's a little bit like me!

Enjoy more great picture books from Bloomsbury Children's Books ...

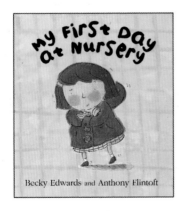

MY FIRST DAY AT NURSERY
Becky Edwards and Anthony Flintoft

BORED CLAUDE
Jill Newton

MUMMY, DON'T GO OUT TONIGHT
Sally Gardner

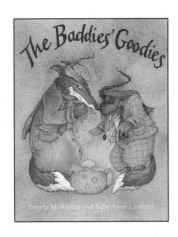

THE BADDIES' GOODIES
Angela McAllister and Sally Anne Lambert

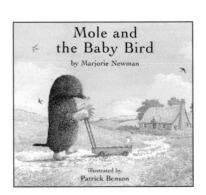

MOLE AND THE BABY BIRD
Marjorie Newman and Patrick Benson

All picture books available in paperback